THE BEST BEEKEEPER OF LALIBELA

A Tale from Africa

by CRISTINA KESSLER

illustrated by

LEONARD JENKINS

Holiday House / New York

Long ago, high in the mountains of
Ethiopia, where purple shadows fill the
valleys and heavy mists hug the hillsides,
the bees arrived in Lalibela.

Some said they came to announce the
birth of a new king, while others
thought only of their honey—sweet, rich,
and golden.

As the centuries passed and the word
spread, villagers poured in from far and
near to buy the sweet nectar.

Each Saturday at the open-air market, a young girl
moved from stall to stall, tasting the honey sellers' wares.

Almaz let the honey drip down her finger like a string of golden diamonds and into her mouth. With a gentle smack of her lips, she said to no one but herself, "It's all very good, but one day mine will be the best."

At the edge of the village, where the forest began, a group of men worked and talked, morning to night. Together they wove long narrow baskets, then placed them high in the pine trees for bees to use as hives.

One day Almaz visited them. "I want to keep bees," she said. "I want to make the best honey in all of Lalibela."

They laughed at her, and the oldest man said, "That's men's work, little girl. Go find your mother and learn to cook and clean and gather firewood. You have a lot of work of your own, so forget bees."

Almaz's eyes filled
with tears. She
turned on her heels
and crashed into a tall,
young priest.

"Slow down, slow down," said
Father Haile Kirros. "What has upset you so?"

"I want to keep bees," she said. "That's all I
want, but they say I can't because I'm a girl and
it is men's work."

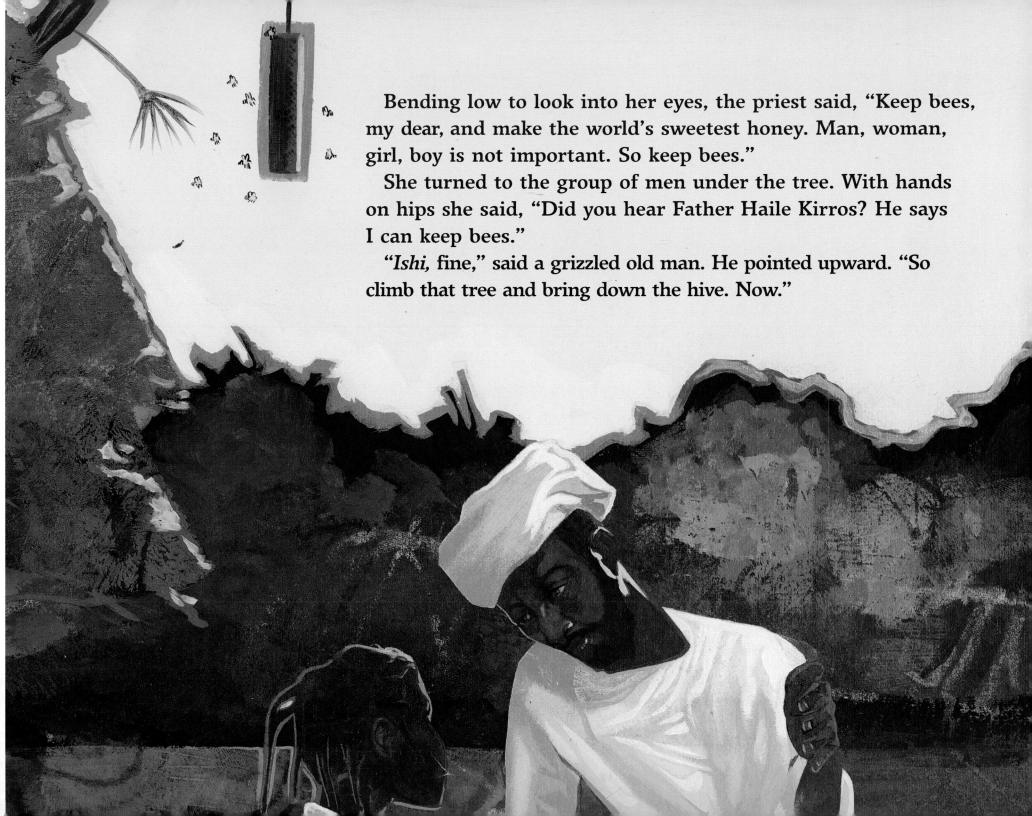

Bending low to look into her eyes, the priest said, "Keep bees, my dear, and make the world's sweetest honey. Man, woman, girl, boy is not important. So keep bees."

She turned to the group of men under the tree. With hands on hips she said, "Did you hear Father Haile Kirros? He says I can keep bees."

"*Ishi,* fine," said a grizzled old man. He pointed upward. "So climb that tree and bring down the hive. Now."

Almaz gazed up and up, to the dangling basket hive. Bees swarmed busily about it. Starting ever so slowly, she inched her way up the tree. Her arms and legs hugged the trunk as tightly as the tree's own bark.

Her big mistake was looking up, then looking down. So far to go, she thought, looking up. And so far to fall, she thought, looking down, while the buzz of bees thundered in her ears.

The men laughed as she scooted down. "Now are you finished? *Baka*? If you can't climb trees, then you can't keep bees. So go and learn the work of women." They patted one another's shoulders as if they'd just won something.

For months they chuckled each time Almaz
passed their tree, saying to one another,
"She's learned her lesson."
But they didn't know Almaz.

Three full moons passed before she appeared at the Saturday morning market again. With delight she laid out a spotless white cloth, carefully smoothing its edges.

And then with pride she lifted a glowing chunk of honeycomb from the can at her side. Drops of honey like golden diamonds dripped in the sunlight.

People gathered at her stall that Saturday and for eight Saturdays to come. Men bought her honey to make *tej,* a frothy honey beer. Women bought it to add to the *genfo,* a porridge they made for their families on cold damp mornings.

They were shocked when she didn't arrive one Saturday. Or the next. Or even the next. On the third Saturday, Father Haile Kirros told her disappointed customers, "I will check on her today."

He found her glaring at a strange mud shape.
"It's my hive," Almaz said, pointing to the
mud cone with four openings sitting on
the ground.

"Aha!" exclaimed the priest. "I've
never seen anything like it before."
Streams of ants marched in and
out of the mud hive head to
heel. There was not a bee
in sight.

Almaz tapped the hive with her toe, saying, "It worked fine until the ants came."

"You'll find a way to fix it," Father Haile Kirros said. "It is great, and all great endeavors require great effort. Who knows, the answer could be something very simple."

Just like a worker bee, Almaz was busy for eleven days. First she dug a moat around the hive, but the water just turned the ground to a muddy mess.

Next she tried to hang the hive like a bell, but it was too heavy.

Then one morning her brother gave her the answer as she was washing clothes at the village tap. He passed by pulling his favorite toy. Bumping along the ground behind him on a string was an old tomato can filled with water.

"That's what I'll do," she said to no one but herself.

For two days the family heard the pounding and the cutting. "Let her be," said her mother, "for she's found the answer."

When the pounding stopped, Almaz raced to the
market square and bought a piece of the sweetest
honeycomb she could find, then placed it inside
her hive.

And then she waited—one day, two, three days,
four—until the bees of Lalibela began to arrive.

When the buzz of the bees filled the
back corner of the family compound
again, Almaz ran to find Father Haile
Kirros. He held on to his wobbly hat as
they rushed down the narrow paths
that led to Almaz's hut.

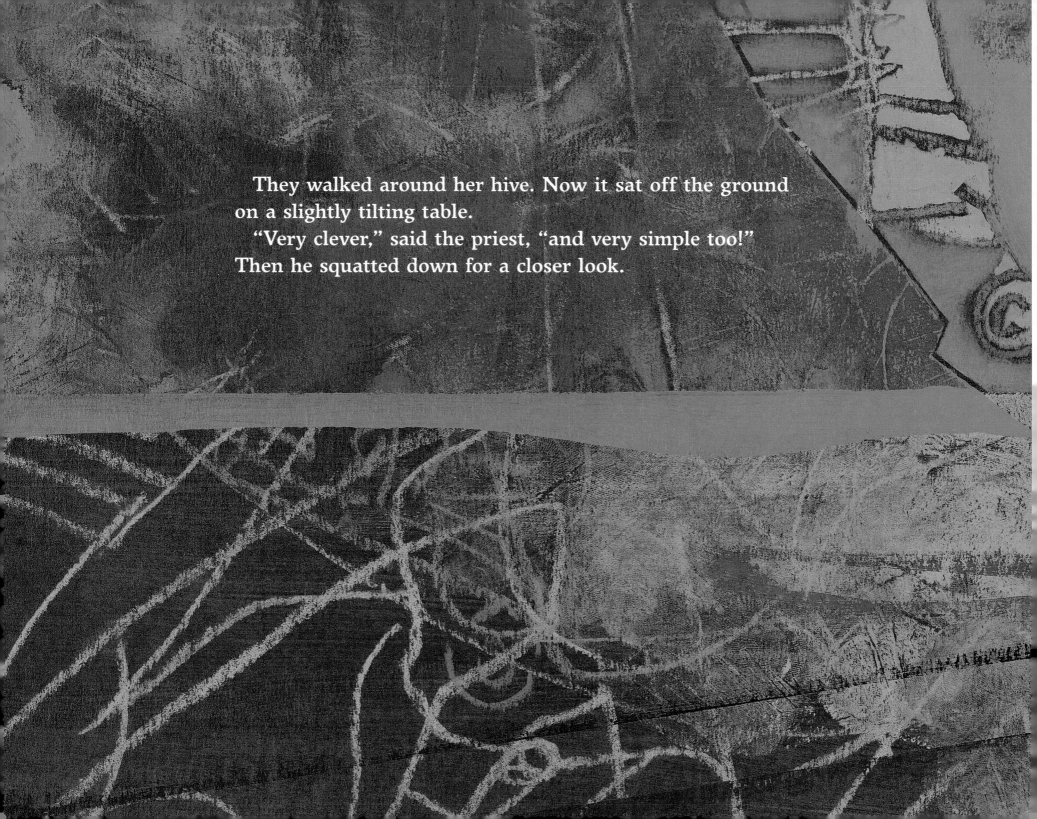

They walked around her hive. Now it sat off the ground on a slightly tilting table.

"Very clever," said the priest, "and very simple too!" Then he squatted down for a closer look.

Crouching beside him, their heads nearly touching, Almaz said, "It works because ants can't swim." The four table legs each stood in an old tomato paste can filled with water. The bees hummed overhead.

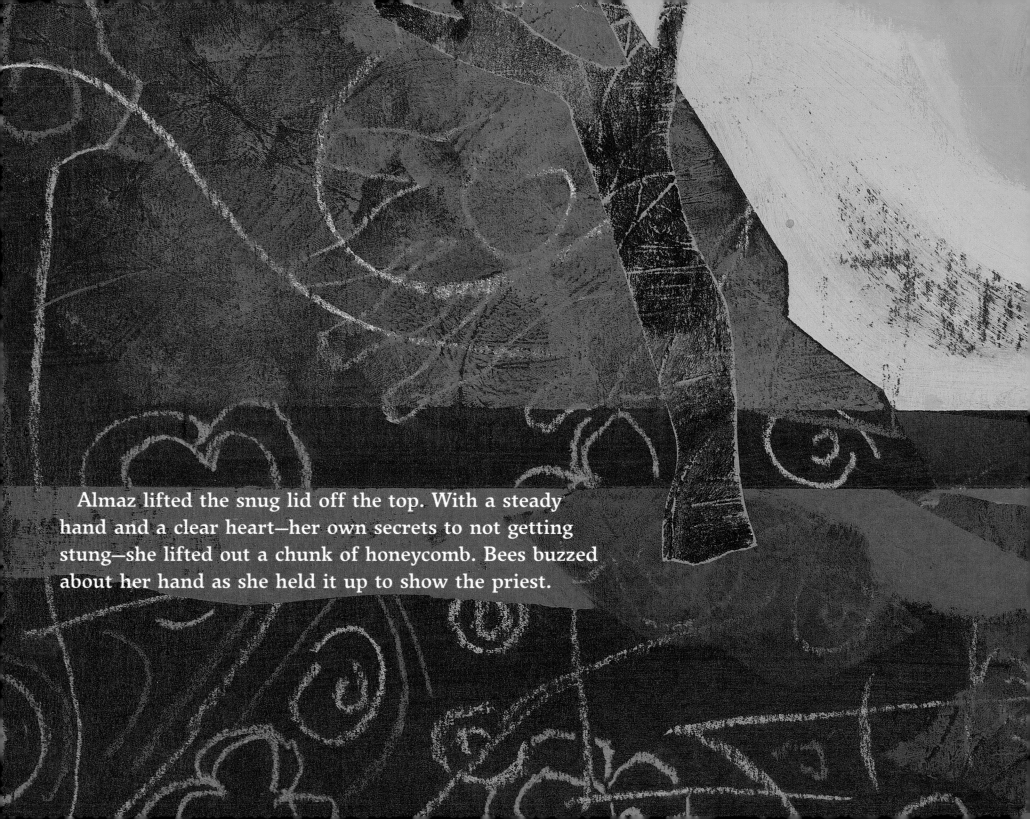

Almaz lifted the snug lid off the top. With a steady hand and a clear heart—her own secrets to not getting stung—she lifted out a chunk of honeycomb. Bees buzzed about her hand as she held it up to show the priest.

By the next full moon, the men watched the line that formed in front of Almaz at the Saturday market. The old one who had sent her up the tree scratched his head. "Who would have thought that she would succeed?"

He led the others through the crowd, right up to her. Clearing his throat to silence the crowd, he said, "Welcome back, Almaz—the best beekeeper of Lalibela."

"*Amessegenallehu,*" she said, thanking them, then let golden honey diamonds drip into her mouth. "Life is sweet," she said with a sticky smile.

Author's Note
THE LEGEND OF LALIBELA

In 1181 a baby boy was born in Roha, Ethiopia. His older brother, Harbay, was destined to be king until a mysterious thing happened.

Legend has it that one day his mother saw the baby lying happily in his cradle, surrounded by a dense swarm of bees. Recalling an old Ethiopian belief that the animal world could foretell the advent of important personages, his mother cried out, "The bees know that this child will become king." She named him Lalibela, which means "the bee recognizes his sovereignty."

King Lalibela ruled for many years, and today visitors flock to the town renamed after him to see for themselves the incredible churches he built, hewed from stone. The churches of Lalibela are often called the Eighth Wonder of the World. It is a mystery how such huge, monolithic structures were carved from rock. It is estimated that about forty thousand people worked to excavate these churches. One church is believed to have been excavated in a day with the help of angels.

This story is set in modern-day Lalibela, which sits at more than five thousand feet in stark, craggy mountains. The honey industry is still very active in the village. Orthodox Ethiopians from all over visit the churches of Lalibela at least once in their lifetime. Almost all who visit leave with a jug of honey, regarded as the sweetest in the country.

Glossary

(Tigringna and Amharic are two of the languages spoken in Ethiopia.)

TIGRINGNA WORDS

almaz (all-moss)—diamond

AMHARIC WORDS

amessegenallehu (ah-ma-sa-ga-na-low)—thank you

baka (ba-kaw)—finished, enough

genfo (gen-fo)—porridge

ishi (i(t)-she)—fine, okay

tej (tedge)—honey beer

To Joe, as always,
and to my good Ethiopian friends Rahel, Shitaye, and Mulu—
amessegenallehu for all your great support.
And to all the young girls of the world—
follow your dreams.
C. K.

For Yaway
L. J.

Amessegenallehu to Solomon Etefa of the Ethiopian Mission
to the United Nations, for all his help.

Library of Congress Cataloging-in-Publication Data
Kessler, Cristina.
The best beekeeper of Lalibela : a tale from Africa / by Cristina Kessler ;
illustrated by Leonard Jenkins.— 1st ed.
p. cm.
Summary: In the Ethiopian mountain village of Lalibela, famous for its churches
and honey, a young girl determines to find a way to be a beekeeper despite being
told that is something only men can do.
ISBN-10: 0-8234-1858-8 (hardcover)
ISBN-13: 978-0-8234-1858-9 (hardcover)
[1. Bee culture—Fiction. 2. Sex role—Fiction. 3. Determination (Personality trait)—
Fiction. 4. Lalibela (Ethiopia)—Fiction. 5. Ethiopia—Fiction.] I. Jenkins, Leonard, ill.
II. Title.

PZ7.K4824Bes 2006
[E]—dc22
2005046217